EVERETT ANDERSON'S
1·2·3

EVERETT ANDERSON'S 1·2·3

by LUCILLE CLIFTON   •   *Illustrations by* ANN GRIFALCONI

HENRY HOLT AND COMPANY • *New York*

Published by Henry Holt and Company, Inc.,
115 West 18th Street, New York, New York 10011.
Published simultaneously in Canada by
Fitzhenry & Whiteside Ltd.,
91 Granton Drive, Richmond Hill, Ontario L4B 2N5.
First published in 1977 by Holt, Rinehart and Winston.
Reissued in 1992 by Henry Holt and Company.

Library of Congress Cataloging-in-Publication Data
Clifton, Lucille.
    Everett Anderson's 1-2-3 / by Lucille Clifton; illustrations by
Ann Grifalconi.
    Summary: As a small boy's mother considers remarriage, he
considers the numbers one, two, and three—sometimes they're lonely,
sometimes crowded, but sometimes just right.
    ISBN 0-8050-2310-0
    [1. Mothers and sons—Fiction.   2. Remarriage—Fiction.   3. Afro-
Americans—Fiction.   4. Stories in rhyme.]   I. Grifalconi, Ann,
ill.   II. Title.   III. Title: Everett Anderson's one-two-three.
[PZ8.3.C573Eu   1992]
[E]—dc20   92-8031

Printed in the United States of America
on acid-free paper. ∞

10 9 8 7 6 5 4 3 2 1

For Darryl, Eric, and Kevin Walker, my friends.
—L. C.

To the family of Three I always loved.
—A. G.

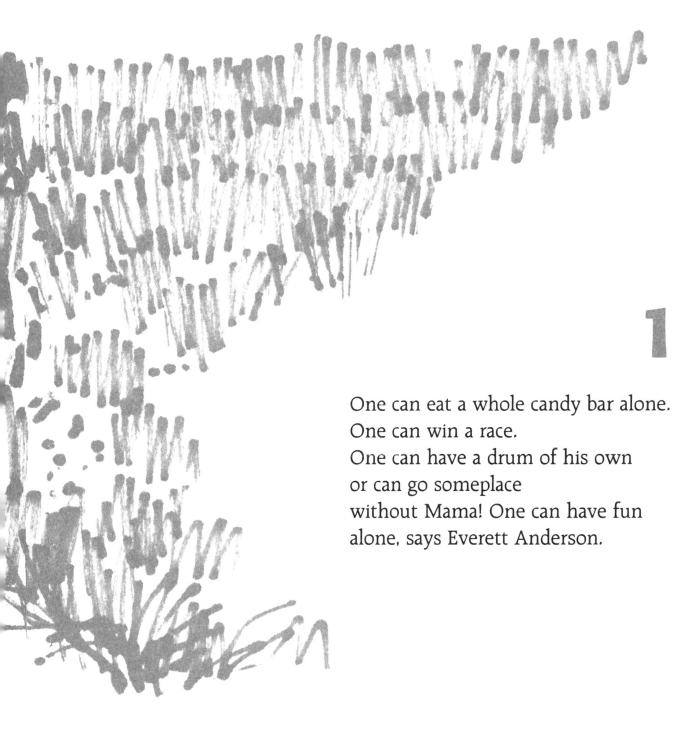

1

One can eat a whole candy bar alone.
One can win a race.
One can have a drum of his own
or can go someplace
without Mama! One can have fun
alone, says Everett Anderson.

A new someone
has come to stay
and be a neighbor to
14A,
Mr. Tom Perry
who drives a bus.
"He might," Mama says,
"be a friend to us."

1

Everett Anderson thinks that One
is a lonely number.
It's not much fun
talking to yourself all day,
and so he tries to understand the way
that Mr. Perry likes to be
talking to Mama a lot lately.

Everett Anderson says, Thank you,
but I have gotten used to Two.
Two at dinner,
Two flying kites,
Two at market,
Two at night, and
I'm not lonely at all, thank you,
I have gotten used to Two.

2

Suppose we stopped being Two?
What would I do?

Everett Anderson worries,
and all the while
Mama keeps smiling
her special smile.

2

"People miss people
when they go.
Everett Anderson,
you must know
I miss your Daddy,"
Mama smiles.

2

"But Two is a lonely
number, too,
sometimes for me and
sometimes for you,
and when things end we
don't just stop,
we keep on being, and
that's the story of
what you're seeing."

3

Everett Anderson's Mama is humming
because Mr. Perry soon is coming.
Sometimes Three is too much to share,
and sometimes Three doesn't fit somewhere,
and Three at dinner crowds the dishes.
Three should be Two! Everett Anderson wishes.

3

Mr. Perry and Everett
go for a walk
because Mr. Perry wants to talk
about Three and Two
and One and other
things, including Everett's mother
and how she is singing every day
and laughing in a brand new way.

Everett Anderson thinks
(he's very bright)
if his Mama is happy
it might be all right.

3

Mr. Perry smiles at Everett Anderson's face
and says, "I can't take your Daddy's place,
but I can be me if you'll give me a chance,
and Three can work and sing and dance
and not make a crowd in 14 A."

3

It's still
hard to get used to Three
Everett thinks, but he thinks
he will.

One can be lonely and One can be fun, and
Two can be awful or perfect for some, and
Three can be crowded or can be just right or
even too many, you have to decide.

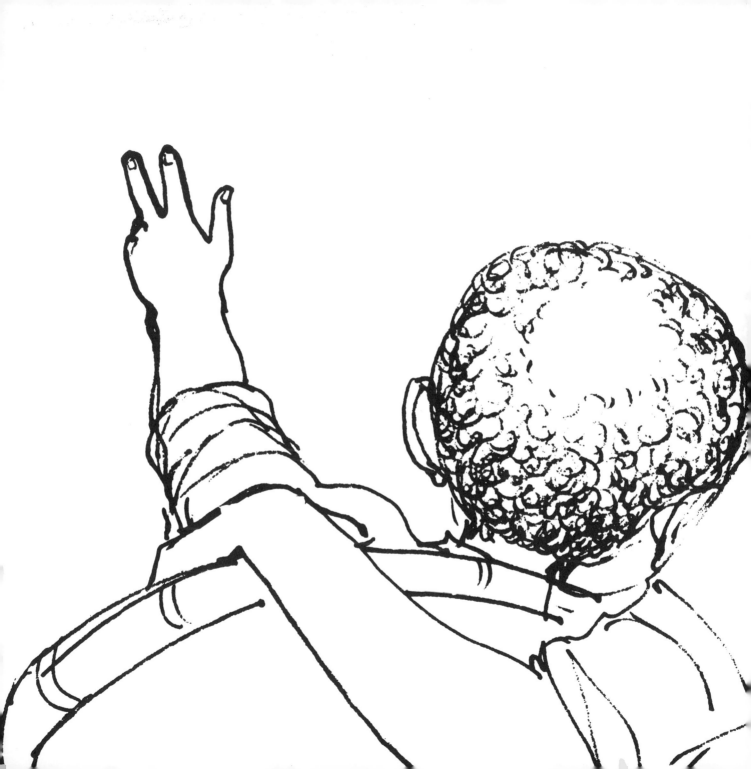

1 2 3

Mr. Perry and Everett Anderson too
know the number you need
is the number for you.